OFF TO SCHOOL!

SIMON SPOTLIGHT
An imprint of Simon & Schuster Children's Publishing Division
1230 Avenue of the Americas, New York, New York 10020
© Peyo - 2003 - Licensed through Lafig Belgium - www.smurf.com
English language translation © Peyo - 2003 - Licensed through Lafig Belgium - www.smurf.com
Originally published in French as *Tous à l'école!*
All rights reserved, including the right of reproduction in whole or in part in any form.
SIMON SPOTLIGHT, READY-TO-READ, and colophon are registered trademarks of Simon & Schuster, Inc.
For information about special discounts for bulk purchases, please contact Simon & Schuster Special Sales
at 1-866-506-1949 or business@simonandschuster.com.
Manufactured in the United States of America 0411 LAK
First Edition
2 4 6 8 10 9 7 5 3 1
ISBN 978-1-4424-2138-7 (pbk)
ISBN 978-1-4424-3062-4 (hc)

OFF TO SCHOOL!

by Peyo

Ready-to-Read

Simon Spotlight

New York   London   Toronto   Sydney

The Smurfs were getting ready for a big party.

"Papa Smurf, how much currant syrup should I smurf to this barrel of water?" asked a Smurf.

"Three cups for every bucket of water," replied Papa Smurf.

"Hmm . . . ," the Smurf said as he tried to figure out how much syrup to add to the barrel.

"There are six buckets of water in the barrel. That means I need sixteen cups of syrup!"

"No," Papa Smurf said. "You need eighteen cups. Three times six is eighteen!"

Another Smurf did not know how to cut a pie into twelve equal slices. "First smurf the pie in two," Papa Smurf said. "Then in two again. After that you just have to cut each piece—"

"In two!" exclaimed the Smurf.
"No . . . in three!" said Papa Smurf.

Papa Smurf was getting annoyed. It looked like the Smurfs had forgotten how to do simple math! Then Greedy and Clumsy showed him the banner they made—and almost every word was spelled wrong!

"That is it!" Papa Smurf cried.
"You are all going back to school!
You need to smurf your basic skills
again."

The Smurfs were shocked. They were one hundred years old! How could they go back to school? But they did what Papa Smurf told them to do.

Papa Smurf went over spelling,
reading, and math. The Smurfs
found it hard—they had forgotten
a lot! But Papa took the time to
explain everything.

The Smurfs tried to listen, but it
was too hard! They did find it easy
to have fun at recess, though!

Poor Greedy Smurf! He could not
think when he was hungry. And
he was always hungry!
But Papa Smurf would not let him
eat in class.

At the end of the school day
Papa Smurf told the Smurfs
that he would not be at school
the next day. Brainy would be
the teacher instead.

Greedy was not happy. "Smurf in class to listen to Brainy talk about the planets and the stars? And not eat for hours?"
Greedy thought he had better things to do.

The next day, Greedy was on his way to school when he decided to run away. He was not going to waste his day listening to Brainy when he could be eating!

Greedy headed into the forest, where he ran from tree to bush, gobbling up blackberries and hazelnuts.

At school, everyone noticed that Greedy was not there. And Brainy was furious!

"I will tell Papa Smurf!" Brainy said.

Papa Smurf was not happy to hear
that Greedy was not at school.
"He will have to skip dessert
tonight," Papa said. "That will teach
him to skip school!"

But when Greedy did not show up
for supper, Papa Smurf got worried.
"If he is not back by the time it is
dark, we will have to smurf for him,"
he said.

Meanwhile, Greedy had lost his way in the forest. He had been walking around for hours as he tried to find his way back home.

When it got too dark to see, Greedy found a place to rest under a rock. "I am so tired," he said. "And I am so hungry, too!"

That night, the sounds of the forest kept Greedy awake. And he tried not to think about being scared. To shut out the sounds and scary thoughts, Greedy began to say the times tables he had been studying at school.

Just as he was about to say, "Five times five is . . ." he heard someone call his name. "Greedy! Greedy!" "Are you out here somewhere?" someone else shouted.

Greedy was so happy!
"Thank you for looking for me,"
Greedy told his friends. "But it is
so dark. How will you know how
to smurf home?"
"Oh, that's easy," Clumsy said.
"Climb this rock and I will show you."
On top of the rock, Clumsy pointed
to the night sky. "Look, there's the
Big Dipper. And there's the North
Star. It always shows the north.
Brainy smurfed us all that in school!"

The next morning, Greedy got up extra early. Now that he knew what important things he could learn at school, he did not want to miss a single day!

But when he got to school the doors were locked! After last night's big adventure, Papa Smurf had decided to give everyone a day off from school.

"Oh, just my luck!" Greedy said.
"Now that I have decided to smurf
hard in school, it's closed!"